No movie. No fun.

Joe spotted something dark under the sofa. He got down on his hands and knees and pulled it out. It was the velvet bag that the videocassette had been in.

"Here it is," he yelled.

"Thanks, Joe," the Great Merlino said. He took the bag and held it up. Everyone could see it was empty. "The magic word is *abracadabra*. Say it with me. Ready?"

Everyone shouted the word together, "Abracadabra!"

Merlino waved his wand over the velvet bag. Then he reached inside.

He frowned again. Then turned the bag inside out. It was empty.

This time the cassette really had vanished!

Frank and Joe Hardy: The Clues Brothers

#1 The Gross Ghost Mystery
#2 The Karate Clue
#3 First Day, Worst Day
#4 Jump Shot Detectives
#5 Dinosaur Disaster
#6 Who Took the Book?
#7 The Abracadabra Case

Available from MINSTREL BOOKS

FRANK AND JOE HARDY: THE CLUES BROTHERS™

THE ABRACADABRA CASE

Franklin W. Dixon

Illustrated by
Marcy Ramsey

A MINSTREL® BOOK

Published by POCKET BOOKS
New York   London   Toronto   Sydney   Tokyo   Singapore

A MINSTREL PAPERBACK *Original*

A Minstrel Book published by
POCKET BOOKS, a division of Simon & Schuster Inc.
1230 Avenue of the Americas, New York, NY 10020

Copyright © 1998 by Simon & Schuster Inc.

Front cover illustration by Thompson Studio

Produced by Mega-Books, Inc.

ISBN: 0-671-00408-5

First Minstrel Books printing July 1998

10 9 8 7 6 5 4 3 2 1

FRANK AND JOE HARDY: THE CLUES BROTHERS is a trademark of Simon & Schuster Inc.

THE HARDY BOYS, A MINSTREL BOOK and colophon are registered trademarks of Simon & Schuster Inc.

Printed in the U.S.A.

1

A Magical Birthday Party

Want to see a magic trick?" Eight-year-old Joe Hardy held up a chocolate-covered peanut. He waved his other hand in front of it.

"I am going to make this piece of candy disappear," he said. Then he popped the peanut in his mouth. "Presto! Gone!"

His nine-year-old brother, Frank, grinned. "Oh, yeah?" he asked. "Why is your cheek sticking out?"

Their friend Chet Morton picked up a handful of peanuts. "I know how to do that trick, only better," he announced. "I am going to make *all* these peanuts disappear!"

Chet shoved all the peanuts into his mouth. He held up his empty hand. It was smeared with chocolate.

Chet's younger sister, Iola, was sitting next to him. She was in second grade. She looked at Chet's hand. "Yuck!" she said. "You are such a mess."

"It takes one to know one," Chet said. He tried to rub chocolate on her cheek. She giggled and pushed his arm away.

It was Saturday afternoon. Brian Ludlow was having a birthday party. He had invited all the kids from karate class.

A girl with short, dark hair walked over to the group of friends. "Hi," Joe said to her. "You're Jennifer, right? I remember you from karate last week."

"That's right," Jennifer told Joe. "It was my first class. I was Brian's guest. We go to the same school."

"Did you like karate?" Iola asked.

"I think so. I don't know for sure yet." Jennifer looked around the room. "What an awesome place! I never saw a TV screen that big. Why is that curtain across the end of the room?"

"We're going to see a magic show," Joe told her. "I can't wait. I'm going to sit up front. Maybe I'll learn how to do some tricks."

"The magician's name is the Great Merlino," Frank added. "He is so cool. He's in high school. Being a magician is his part-time job."

"Big deal," a voice cut in. "Magic shows are for babies. So you babies should love it."

Joe looked over his shoulder. He already knew who that voice belonged to. Zack Jackson was in Frank's fourth-grade class. He had wild black hair. On his hand was a rub-on tattoo of a spider. His hobby was pushing other kids around.

"Watch out, Zack," Joe said. "What if Merlino turns you into a toad?"

"I wish he would," Chet said in a low voice.

"Hey, cut it out," Biff Hooper growled. He was a really big kid with blond hair. He was part of Zack's gang, the Zack Pack. The gang had been named by Joe's friend Mike Mendez. Mike was in Joe's class.

"Take it easy, guys," Frank said. He stepped between Biff and Chet. "This is a party, remember?"

Brian was sitting next to the window. He had begun to open his presents. "Hey, everybody! Come see what I got," he called. He was holding up a videocassette.

"What is that?" Joe asked. He walked over to get a closer look. "A movie?"

"It's the new Jimmy Han movie—*The Dragon's Cave*," Brian said.

Everybody in karate class loved Jimmy Han. Jimmy was an incredible kung fu fighter. He did all his own stunts.

Tanya Wilkins pushed her way to the front of the group. She loved karate, and

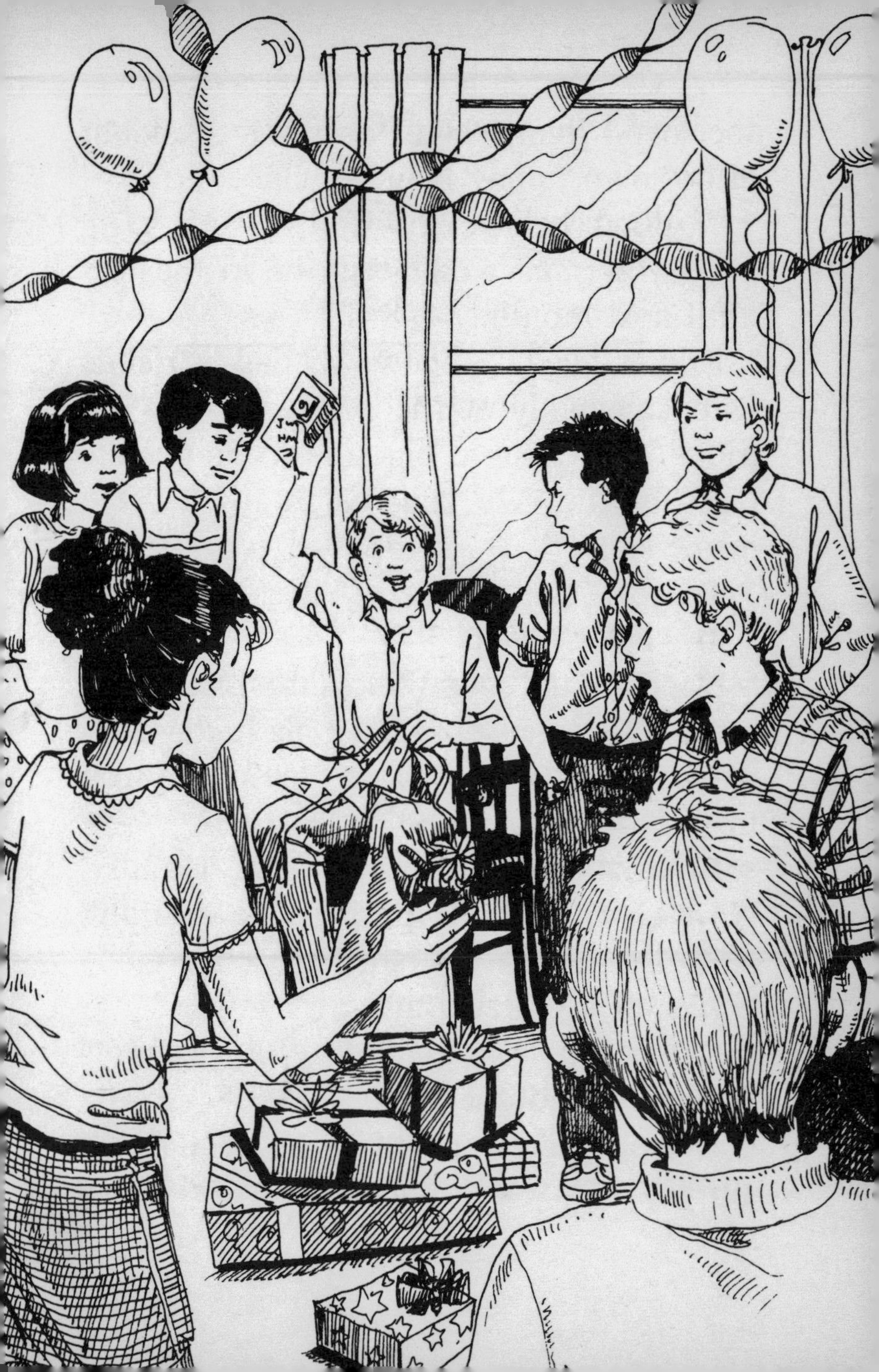

she loved Jimmy Han. She was president of her own Jimmy Han fan club.

"I don't believe it," Tanya said. *"The Dragon's Cave* won't even be in theaters until next month."

Brian smiled. "I know. My dad is friends with somebody at the movie studio. His friend knows I'm a big fan. So he got the tape for me. We can watch it after the magic show."

Tanya's face lit up. "Awesome," she said. "I can't wait."

"Um, Brian?" Jennifer said. "Listen. My brother's home sick. He's a big Jimmy Han fan, too. Can I borrow the tape? He'd love to see it."

Brian shook his head. "Sorry, Jennifer. No way. Dad had to promise we wouldn't lend it to anyone. What if someone made copies of it? They'd make a fortune."

"And Jimmy would *lose* a fortune," Tanya pointed out.

A teenager came out from behind the curtain. He was tall and had dark hair.

Frank nudged Joe. "Look," he said. "That's the Great Merlino."

"Brian?" the Great Merlino said. "We'll be starting in five minutes. Can you get people to sit down?"

"I'll try," Brian said. "Why not just cast a sitting spell?"

Merlino smiled. "What if I didn't remember how to take it away? Five minutes, okay?"

He turned to go. Frank walked over and tapped him on the arm. "Mr. Merlino? I'm Frank Hardy. My brother, Joe, and I want to learn magic. Do you give lessons?"

"Sometimes I do, Frank," Merlino said. "Right now I'm very busy with birthday parties. Maybe we can work something out. Talk to me after the show."

"Great!" Frank said. He looked over at Joe and grinned.

Everyone moved toward the stage. A sofa and some chairs were lined up near the front. Joe and Frank hurried over. But all the places were already taken.

"Let's sit on the floor," Frank suggested. "We'll still see okay."

There was a blast of trumpet music from a tape recorder behind the curtain. The curtain slid aside. In the center of the stage area was a small, round table with a black velvet cover. A bright light shone down on the table. Behind it, in the shadows, was another table. It was loaded with mysterious-looking equipment.

"Ooh!" Everyone in the audience gasped.

The Great Merlino walked onstage. Now he was wearing a long, black cape and a tall top hat. He looked much bigger, much older, and *much* more magical, Joe thought.

Merlino took off his hat. Frank and Joe could see there was nothing in it. Then Merlino reached inside and pulled out a bouquet of flowers. Everybody clapped.

"Thank you," the Great Merlino said. "Welcome to an afternoon of mystifying prestidigitation."

"That means magic," Joe whispered.

"That's right, young man," Merlino said to Joe. "How would you like to help me with the next trick?"

"Yes!" Joe said. He stood up and walked to the stage.

The Great Merlino took out a deck of cards. "Pick any card you like," he said to Joe. "Don't tell me what it is. And don't let me see it."

Joe took a card from the middle of the deck. It was the seven of hearts.

"Show it to everybody," Merlino said.

Joe turned around. He held the card up high so that everybody could see it.

"Put it back with the others," Merlino told him.

The deck was now inside a big glass bowl. Joe slipped his card in near the middle. What was going to happen? he wondered.

The Great Merlino lifted the bowl in his left hand. He held a black wand in his right hand. He tapped the wand on the glass three times.

"Abracadabra, ali-kazan. What was the card in Joe's hand?"

Joe's eyes widened. He felt the hair on the back of his neck stand up. One of the cards was slowly rising out of the deck. But how? Merlino's hand was nowhere near it.

"It's magic!" Joe said.

The card turned in midair so that everyone could see what it was. Joe gasped. It was the seven of hearts. The same card that he had picked!

2

Vanishing Act

Is this your card?" Merlino asked. He grabbed the card and handed it to Joe.

Joe nodded. "It sure is."

Everybody clapped. Everybody but Zack. "Joe told him what the card was," Zack said loudly.

"Did not," Joe said. "And suppose I had? What made it pop up?"

"Mirrors," Zack replied. "These tricks are always done with mirrors. Or strings."

Joe laughed and went back to his seat. He knew there were no mirrors or strings

11

holding up the card. But how had the Great Merlino done it? he wondered.

"Is everyone ready for the next trick?" Merlino called.

"Yes!" everyone shouted.

Frank leaned forward. This time he was going to see how the trick was done, he decided.

Merlino held up up a rope. One end section was red, the middle section was white, and the other end was blue.

Frank narrowed his eyes and looked at the rope carefully. He could see a knot between the red section and the white section of the rope. There was another knot between the white section and the blue section.

"I think there are three ropes," Frank whispered to Joe. "And Merlino tied them together."

"Who knows how to jump rope?" Merlino asked.

Iola waved her hand. "Me, me!" she

called. Rudy, a boy who was also in second grade, shouted even louder.

Merlino looked all around the room. Then he pointed to Tanya. She jumped up and went to the front.

Merlino asked Tanya her name. Then he said, "Well, Tanya, you couldn't jump rope with these ropes, could you?"

"No," Tanya said. "The knots would get in the way."

"Let me fix that," Merlino said. Slowly he wrapped the rope around his left hand. "I'll need some magic woofle dust," he said. He reached into his pocket. Then he sprinkled something on the rope. "Now, Tanya. When I count to three, blow on the ropes. Ready? One . . . two . . . three!"

Tanya puffed out her cheeks and blew. Merlino unwound the rope. He gave one end to Tanya and stretched out the rope. The knots were gone! Instead of three pieces of rope, there was just one. One end was red, and the other was blue. The part in the middle was white.

Everyone clapped. "He switched ropes," Biff called out.

"Who here has really sharp eyes?" Merlino asked.

Both Rudy and Iola waved their hands wildly. Merlino didn't seem to notice. He pointed to Zack. "Would you like to help me?"

"Fat chance," Frank muttered to Joe. "I'll bet he tries to ruin the trick."

Zack went up to the front. He smirked at his friends sitting in the back.

Merlino held up three big cards. Each one had a different color circle on it. One circle was red, another was yellow, and the third was blue.

"This is called Follow the Red," Merlino said. "I'll turn the cards facedown. Then I'll move them around. Do you think you can keep track of the red card?"

"Sure I can," Zack said.

Frank nudged Joe. "Look," he whispered. "The red card has a bent corner."

"I'll bet Zack saw that, too," Joe whispered back.

Merlino slowly moved the cards around on a small table. Then he stopped. He asked, "Which one is the red card?"

Zack grinned. He pointed to the one with the bent corner. Merlino turned it over and held it up. The circle on it was blue. Zack's jaw dropped in surprise.

"Oops! I guess it's one of the others," Merlino said. "Try again."

Zack pointed to another card. Merlino held it up. This one had a yellow circle.

"Oh, bad luck," Merlino said. "Do you want another chance?"

"It has to be that one," Zack said, pointing at the third card. He sounded angry. "It's the only one left!"

Merlino held up the card. Instead of a circle, there were words: " 'Sorry, wrong again,' " Merlino read.

Everybody laughed. Zack scowled and stomped back to his seat.

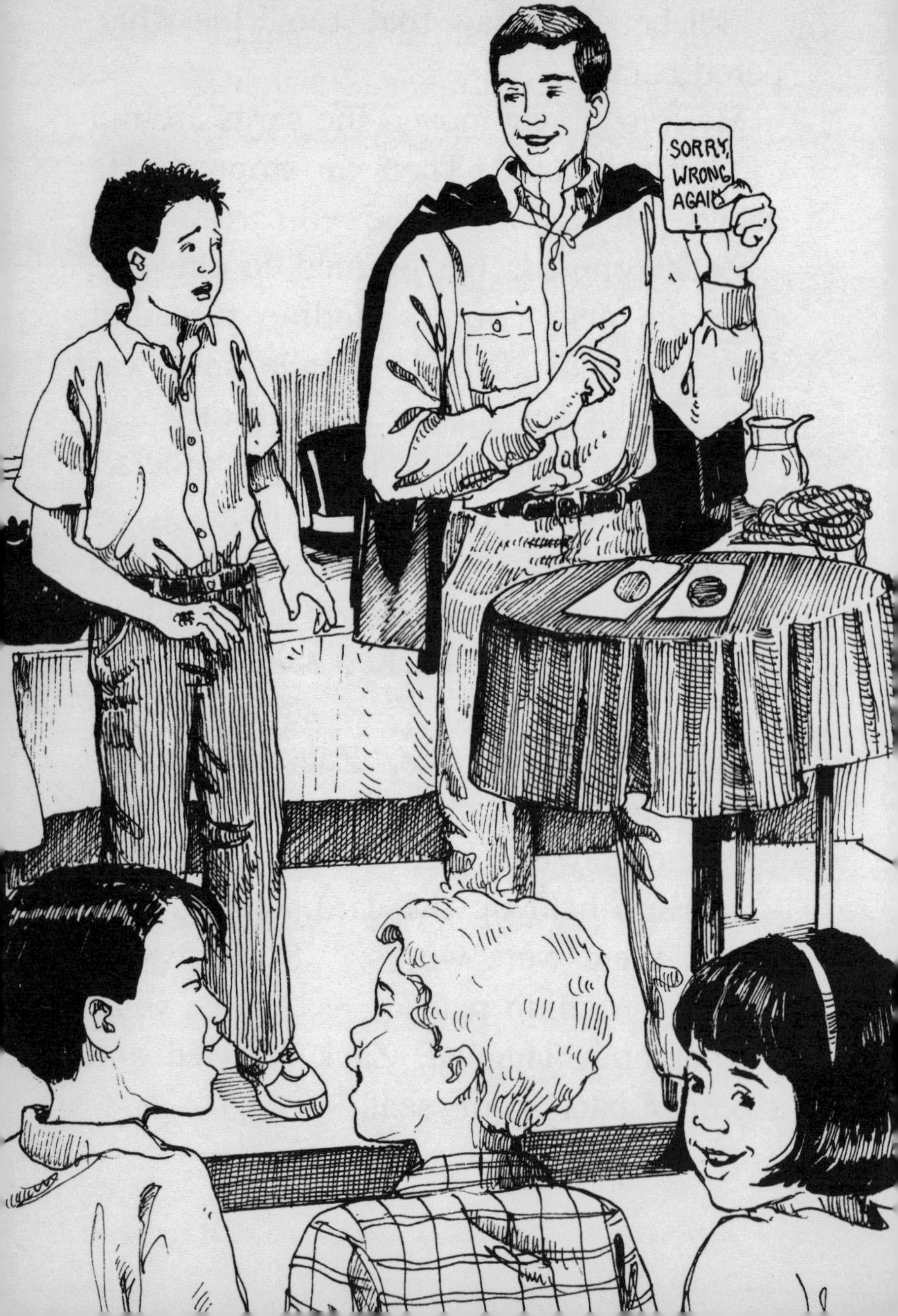
SORRY, WRONG AGAIN!

"Brian," the Great Merlino said. "May I borrow your new Jimmy Han tape?"

"Um, I guess so," Brian said. He brought it up to the stage. "Be really careful with it," he said.

The magician held up a black velvet bag. He showed the audience that it was empty. He took the tape from Brian and put it inside. Then he waved his wand over the bag.

Merlino held the bag upside down. A lemon fell out. He turned the bag inside out. The cassette was not there. It had vanished!

"Oh, well," he said. "Sorry, Brian. I guess that movie's a real lemon."

"Brian looks upset," Joe whispered to Frank. "I hope he gets his movie back."

Merlino put down the velvet bag. He went to the side of the room and picked up a glass and a pitcher full of milk. Suddenly all the lights went out.

Somebody near Joe yelled. Somebody

else started giggling. Joe could hear people moving around.

"Ouch! That's my foot!" a voice shouted. It sounded to Joe like Iola.

"Everybody stay where you are," Brian's father called. He had just come in from the dining room. "I'll get the lights."

A moment later the lights came on. "That wasn't funny," Brian's father said sternly. "Somebody could have gotten hurt."

"Somebody hurt *me*," Iola said. She rubbed her toes.

"I'm really thirsty," Merlino said. He poured a glass of milk from the pitcher and took a sip. Then he poured the rest of the milk into a brass pot. Reaching into the pot, he pulled out a long scarf. It was dry.

"We should call him the *Amazing* Merlino," Frank said to Joe. "I hope he'll agree to teach us some tricks."

Merlino reached high over his head. A coin appeared between his fingers. He tossed it in the brass pot. It clanged loudly.

He reached out to the side. Another coin appeared. That rattled into the pot, too.

He walked out into the audience. He reached behind Frank's ear and pulled a coin out of thin air. He found another in Tanya's hair and another under Chet's chin. They all went clattering into the pot.

Merlino walked over to where Brian was sitting. He put his hand in Brian's shirt pocket and pulled out a coin. He looked at it. Then he said, "I guess this is yours."

Brian took the coin. "Hey, cool!" he shouted. "It's got my name and Happy Birthday on it!"

The kids near Brian crowded around to see. Merlino went to the back of the stage. He stopped at the table and frowned.

"Something's wrong," Joe whispered.

"I think it's the velvet bag," Frank whispered back. "I saw him put it on the table. But it's not there now."

"Well," Merlino said, "sometimes magic things happen. My black bag has flown away. Can anybody find it for me?"

Frank and Joe stood up and looked around. The other kids started looking, too. The black bag wasn't anywhere in sight.

Joe spotted something dark under the sofa. He got down on his hands and knees and pulled it out. It was the velvet bag.

"Here it is," he yelled.

"Thanks, Joe," Merlino said with a grin. He took the bag and held it up. Everyone could see it was empty. "The magic word is *abracadabra*. Say it with me. Ready?"

Everybody shouted the word together. "Abracadabra!"

Merlino waved his wand over the velvet bag. Then he reached inside.

He frowned again. Then he turned the bag inside out. It was still empty.

This time the cassette really had vanished!

3

Searching in Vain

On to my next trick!" the Great Merlino said, and bowed. He put the velvet bag down on the table. Then he picked up a set of silver rings.

"I think he messed up that trick," Frank said to Joe.

"You can't make metal pass through metal," Merlino was saying. "We all know that. But if you know the right words to say . . ."

He held up one ring in his right hand. He banged it loudly against the other two.

"Passe-partout!" he said. Then he let them dangle. Now the three rings were linked like a chain.

The kids clapped but not as much as before. Frank could hear kids whispering to one another. He turned to Joe.

"Where is Brian's cassette?" he murmured. "That wasn't part of the act."

"It's not under the sofa," Joe replied. "I looked there. I would have seen it."

Merlino did another trick with the rings. Only a few kids clapped.

"Hey, wait a second," Brian called. "Where's my Jimmy Han movie? I want it back!"

"Yeah. Let's see the movie," Zack said. "This magic stuff is for babies. We want some kung fu! *Hai-ee-ya!*"

Joe thought that Merlino looked nervous. "Don't worry, Brian," he said. "We'll find your cassette. Now watch carefully."

He held up the three rings. Each one was linked with both of the others. He took one ring in each hand. "One, two, three . . . *Passe-partout!*"

Merlino held up his arms. He still had a ring in each hand. But now all of the rings were separated. The middle ring started to fall. Merlino stuck out his leg and caught it on his foot.

Frank and Joe started clapping. Other kids joined them. Merlino bowed. Then he hurried offstage.

"What about my cassette?" Brian shouted. "What did you do with it?"

Brian's father went over to him. He put his hand on Brian's shoulder and said something softly. Brian nodded. "Okay, Dad," he said.

Merlino came back out front. He had taken off his cape and hat.

"Is the cassette really gone?" Frank asked. "Can we help you look?"

"Thanks, Frank," Merlino said. He made a face. "I think I do need some help. This has never happened before."

23

"Come on, guys," Joe called. "Let's search the room."

All the kids started looking around. Joe got down on the floor and looked under the sofa again. Rudy crawled behind the big TV. He came out with a pencil, four pennies, and a purple paper clip. No cassette, though.

"I give up," Frank said. "It's not here."

"We should search Merlino's stuff," Brian said. "I'll bet that's where it is."

"I'm sorry," Merlino said. "You can't. My equipment is secret. But the cassette isn't there. Believe me. If it was, I'd give it back."

Brian's father clapped his hands. "Listen, everybody," he said. "There's cake and ice cream in the next room."

"Hooray!" Everybody yelled as they crowded through the door. Frank stayed, though. He got down on his hands and knees and crawled behind a big chair. The cassette has to be here somewhere, he thought.

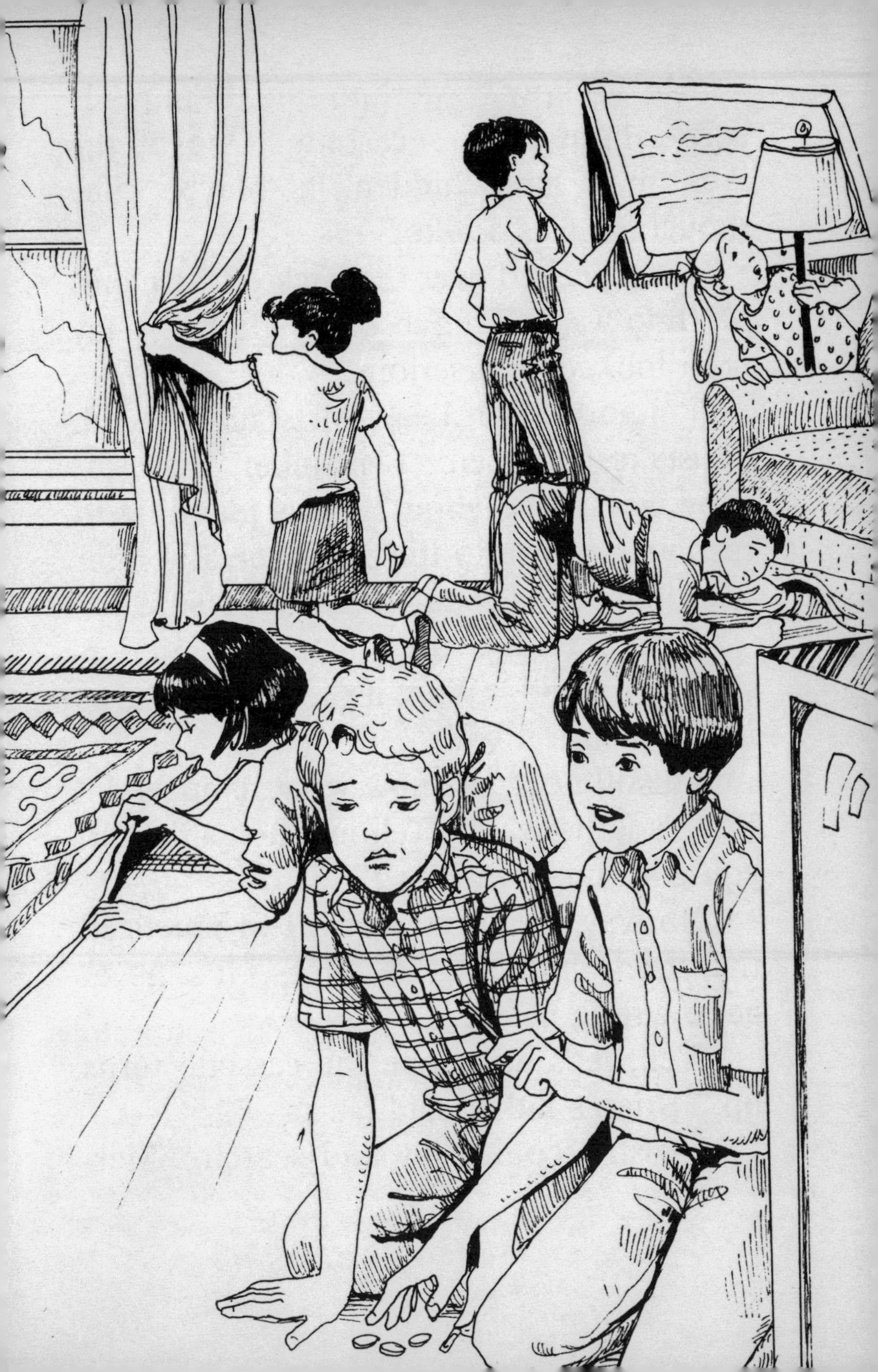

"Mr. Ludlow?" Merlino said. "I'm really sorry about Brian's cassette. One of the kids may have hidden it. Maybe they thought it was a joke."

Frank peeked over the back of the chair. Merlino was talking to Brian's father. They both looked very serious.

"I'm sorry, too, Lee," Mr. Ludlow said. "Mistakes happen. Remember that TV show I told you about? I was planning to recommend you to the producer. But after what happened today, I'm not so sure."

Merlino took a deep breath. "I understand," he said. "What if the cassette turns up? I'm sure it will."

"I'd still need to know what happened," Brian's father said. "Tell me the truth. Did you goof up, somehow?"

"No way," Merlino said. "I've practiced that trick hundreds of times. It's never gone wrong before."

"Well, let's just hope the cassette turns up," Brian's father said.

"I wish I could stay and search," Merlino said. He glanced at his watch. "I can't, though. I have to pack up and leave. I'm performing at another party."

"I see. Well, good luck. Oh—and this is for you." Mr. Ludlow handed Merlino an envelope. "Here's your payment. I enjoyed the show . . . all but the disappearing cassette."

"Same here," Merlino said. He walked over to the stage. Frank stood up and followed.

"Mr. Merlino?" Frank said. "My brother and I love to solve crimes. We're good at it, too. The other kids call us the Clues Brothers. How about if we solve the mystery of Brian's cassette?"

Merlino was packing his equipment in an old suitcase. He paused. "I wish you could, Frank," he said. "It would mean a lot to me. But I'm afraid there's not much chance."

"Why not?" Frank demanded. "Somebody must know something. They might not tell a grown-up, but they'll tell us."

Merlino thought it over. "Do your parents know that you and your brother are detectives?" he asked. "Is it all right with them?"

"Oh, sure," Frank said. "Our dad is a private detective. He gives us advice about our cases. My dad says that my brother and I are following in his footsteps."

"I see," Merlino said. He was smiling. "Okay, then. Anything you can find out will be a big help. Just when I thought I was getting a big break . . ." He shook his head sadly.

"We'll do our best," Frank promised. He walked quickly to the dining room. Joe was standing near the window. Brian and Chet were talking to him. Frank joined them.

"You didn't have any cake," Brian said.

"What's the matter? Don't you want any?" Chet asked. "I'll eat your piece for you."

Frank grinned. "That's okay, Chet.

Brian, what if Joe and I find out what happened to your Jimmy Han cassette?"

"Oh, boy!" Chet said loudly. "The Clues Brothers to the rescue!"

The other kids turned to look. Joe's cheeks turned red.

"I'm their associate," Chet added. "I'm a detective-in-training."

"I wish you would help," Brian told Frank and Joe. "I want my cassette back. And I like Merlino. I don't think it's his fault."

"Where do we start?" Chet asked.

"Somebody switched off the lights," Joe said. "That must have been when the magic bag got taken. Let's figure out who could have gotten to the lights. Frank and I were sitting down when the lights went out. What about you, Brian?"

"I didn't take my own cassette!" Brian said angrily.

"Calm down," Frank said. "A good detective has to check on everybody."

"Okay. I was sitting down, too," Brian said.

"Yeah. Me, too," Chet said.

"Let's ask some more kids," Frank said to Joe.

Tanya and Jennifer were nearby. Joe and Frank went over. "Where were you when the lights went out?" Joe asked.

"Is this a riddle?" Tanya asked. "Do I get a prize for the right answer?"

"We're trying to figure out who turned them out," Frank explained.

"Well, it wasn't me," Tanya said. "I was sitting down near the front."

"And I was next to her," Jennifer said.

"Did anybody get up before the lights went out?" Joe asked.

"Hmmm." Jennifer rubbed her ear. "Oh, sure! When Merlino made the cassette vanish, somebody walked in front of me. I missed the end of the trick. That's why I remember. I was so angry!"

"Who was it?" Frank asked.

"Well . . ." Jennifer stopped for a moment. Then she said, "It was your friend over there—Chet."

"You're sure?" Joe asked.

"Of course I am," Jennifer said. "He got up and left. And he didn't come back for a while. He came back in after the lights came on again."

Frank and Joe looked at each other. Chet had just told them he'd been sitting down. Why had he lied to them? Was he hiding something?

4

An Impossible Crime

Okay, thanks," Joe said to Jennifer. He and Frank walked away from the two girls.

In a low voice, Joe said, "Why didn't Chet tell us the truth?"

"I don't know," Frank replied. "We'd better ask him."

Chet was back in the movie room. "Hi, guys," he said. "How's it going?"

"We're finding out some things," Frank said. "You know when the lights went out? Where did you say you were?"

"I said I was sitting down," Chet told him. He twisted his fingers together.

"Were you really?" Joe asked.

Chet cleared his throat. "Well . . . no. I wasn't."

"Then why did you say you were?" Frank asked. "And where were you really?"

Chet's face turned pink. "I started feeling hungry," he said. He looked down at the floor. "So I decided to check out the refreshments. I sneaked into the dining room. But I didn't take the movie. Honest."

"Did you turn out the lights?" Joe asked.

Chet gave him a puzzled look. "Of course not. Why would I do that? Besides, I was in the dining room when the lights went out. It was pretty scary in the dark. I was afraid I'd knock something over."

Frank looked around. The light switches were next to the door to the movie room. "Did you see anybody near the switches when you walked back into the room?"

"Sure," Chet said. "Brian's dad. He turned the lights back on. Oh, you mean before? No. No one."

"How about on your way to the dining room?" Joe asked. "Was anybody hanging around back there?"

Chet thought hard. "No," he said. "Everybody was up front, watching the show."

"You didn't walk past anybody?" Frank asked.

Chet thought some more. "Umm . . . yes. Biff. He was at the back of the crowd. I remember he gave me a funny look. Maybe he guessed I was going to sneak some food."

"Maybe he thought *you'd* guessed what *he* was doing," Joe said.

"Let's ask him," Frank suggested.

They glanced around. Some kids were already leaving. Biff and Zack were near the door with Biff's mother. Mrs. Hooper was thanking Brian's father.

"We'll have to catch Biff at karate on Tuesday," Joe said.

Frank nodded. "Unless we've solved the mystery by then," he said.

"You could call him," Chet said.

"Not bad for a detective-in-training," Frank said. "There's Dad at the door. It's time to go. Get Iola, will you?"

Mr. Hardy was talking to Brian's father. Frank heard the word "cassette." He could guess what they were talking about.

"Dad? Mr. Ludlow?" Frank said. "Joe and I are already on the case."

"Are you?" Brian's father said. "Thanks, Frank. I appreciate your help, but—"

"I wanted to ask you," Frank said quickly. "Can we come over tomorrow? We'd like to reconstruct the crime."

"Fine," Brian's father said. "How about after lunch? And bring your suits. It may warm up. You could go for a swim."

The next day Frank and Joe rode their bikes over to the Mortons' house. Chet and Iola were waiting on the sidewalk.

Joe glanced at the cloudy sky. "Not much chance of a swim," he said.

"Who cares?" Iola said. "Being a detective is much more exciting than swimming."

"Does she have to tag along?" Chet demanded.

"Iola's been a lot of help in our cases," Frank pointed out. "She's a member of the team."

Iola stuck her tongue out at her brother. "Nyah! So there!"

"Enough chitchat," Joe said. "Let's ride!"

Ten minutes later they were pushing their bikes up Brian's driveway. Below them, they could see the bay filled with sailboats.

"Brian's dad must have lots of boats," Chet said. "He owns the marina, after all. Maybe he'll take us out sailing sometime."

Brian answered the door. "My dad had to go out," he explained. He led them back

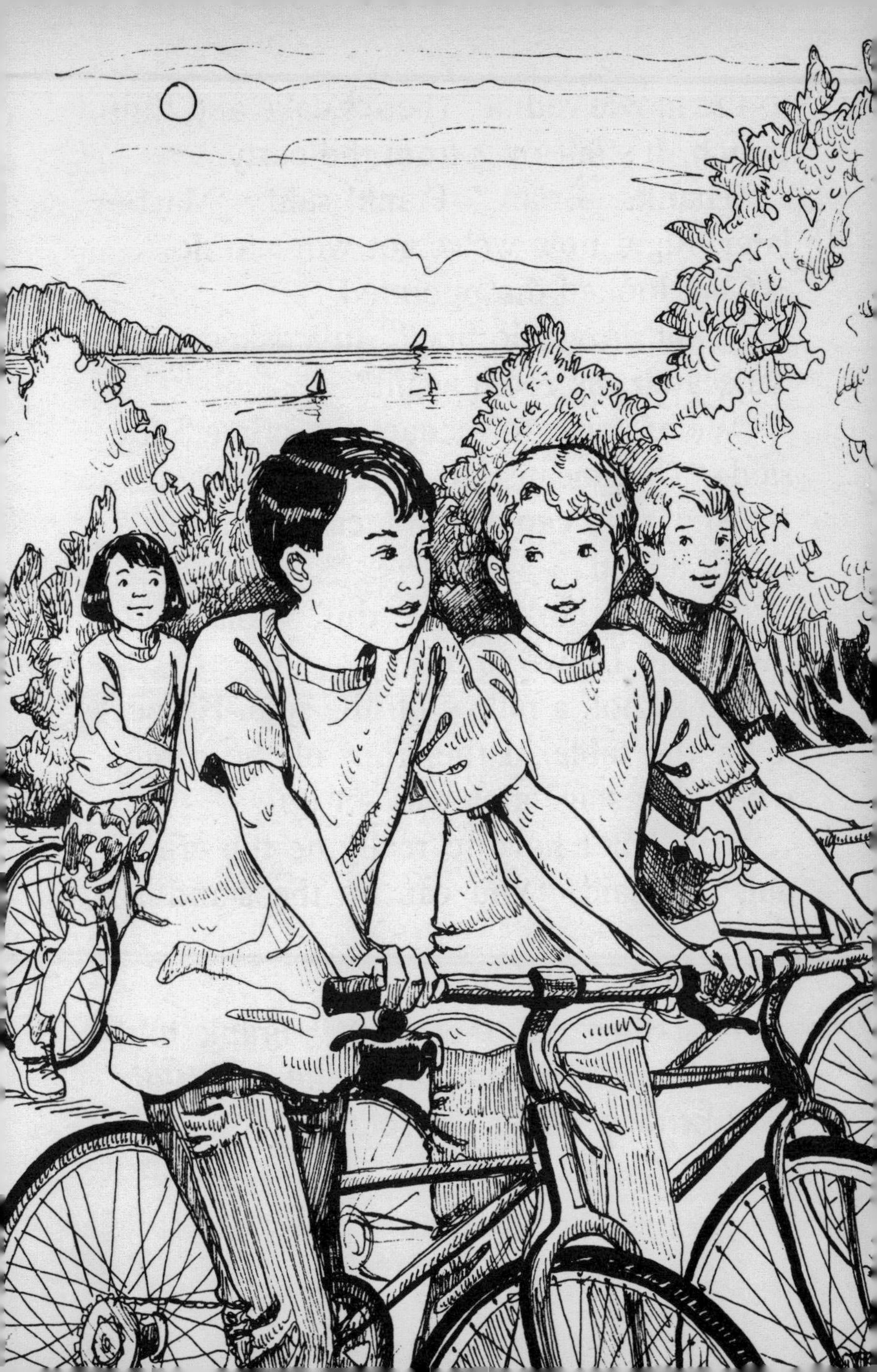

to the movie room. "There's cake and fruit punch. It's left over from the party."

"Thanks, Brian," Frank said. "Maybe later. Right now we've got work to do."

Chet looked disappointed.

"What do we do first?" Iola asked. "Do we search the room again?"

"We're going to reenact the crime," Joe said. "That means, do it over again."

"And you can be the criminal, Iola," Frank added.

"I don't think I like this," Iola said. "What do I have to do?"

Frank took a pillow off the sofa. He put it on the table in the front of the room, where the stage area was set up.

"You don't have to really *be* the criminal," he said. "You can be the stand-in. Okay?"

"A-okay," Iola said.

"First turn out the lights," Frank told Iola. "Then come up here. Take the pillow and throw it under the sofa."

"Why?" Iola asked.

"The pillow is Merlino's magic bag," Joe explained. "I'll be Brian's dad and turn the lights back on."

Iola nodded. "I get it. Okay, here goes."

She walked to the back of the room. Click! The room went dark. A few seconds later something clattered to the floor.

"Ouch!" Iola said. "That hurt!"

Joe counted to fifteen, then switched on the lights. Iola was still in the center of the room. She looked angry.

"I didn't even get to the front," she said. "I kept bumping into things."

"That's what I thought would happen," Frank said. "You see what that means?"

"Sure," Joe replied. "It's an impossible crime."

"But it happened," Brian said.

"What if—" Iola began. She stopped.

"Go ahead," Frank told her.

"What if one kid turned out the lights and somebody else took the bag?" she said.

"A conspiracy!" Chet said in a spooky-sounding voice.

"Maybe," Frank said. He looked around. "But why couldn't we find the cassette?"

"The bag was under the sofa," Iola said. "I'll bet the cassette is under the cushions."

"We looked yesterday," Chet said.

"We should look again," Iola said. "Maybe we missed something." She went to the sofa and lifted the cushions. There was nothing there.

"See, smarty?" Chet said.

"Wait, this is a sofa bed," Iola said. "One time I lost a book inside the sofa bed in our den. I didn't find it until the next time we used the bed."

Frank looked at Joe. They took the cushions off the sofa. Joe grabbed the handle at the front and tugged. The mattress lifted up and unfolded.

"My Jimmy Han cassette!" Brian exclaimed. "There it is!"

5

Motives to Go

I'm confused," Joe told Frank and Chet. "We've found out a lot. But what does it all mean?"

It was recess on Monday morning. The three friends were talking in the schoolyard.

"Why not drop it?" Chet suggested. "After all, we found Brian's cassette."

Iola was passing by with her friend Brad. She heard what Chet said. " 'We'?" she said. "*I* found it. So there!" She walked on.

"Little sisters," Chet muttered.

"We can't drop it," Frank said. He explained about Merlino and the TV show. "Besides, the Clues Brothers always solve their cases."

"So who hid the cassette?" Joe said. "And why? What was the motive?"

"Zack was mad at Merlino for making him look silly," Chet said. "Maybe he wanted to get even."

Frank nodded. "Maybe. Then there's Jennifer. She wanted to borrow the cassette. Brian said no. What if she decided to take it anyway? Then she got scared and hid it in the sofa."

"Tanya's really proud of her Jimmy Han collection," Chet said. "I'll bet she'd do anything to have that cassette in it."

"Even steal?" Joe said. "You know how Tanya's always saying things that Jimmy Han says in his movies. Things like 'Honesty is more valuable than gold.' Besides, there's someone else who was mad at Merlino. Iola kept putting her hand up. He never called on her. And she was the one who found it the second time we searched the movie room. What if Iola took the tape?"

Chet turned red. "No way, Joe," he said. "My sister might be an annoying pest sometimes. But she's not a thief. Just forget it."

"I didn't say she did it," Joe said. "But she might have. She had a motive."

"Lots of people did," Frank pointed out. "That tape is worth a lot. But remember, it wasn't taken, just hidden."

"What about this?" Joe said. "Whoever took the tape wanted to make Merlino look bad."

"Or meant to steal it but chickened out," Frank said.

"Or maybe *one* person chickened out," Joe said. "Maybe someone turned the lights out and the other person got scared and didn't take the tape."

"The Zack Pack!" Chet said. "Come on.

Let's see what Zack and his gang have to say about this."

The bell rang. Recess was over. Chet and the Hardys started for the entrance.

"We'll have to catch them at lunch," Frank said.

At noon Frank and Chet waited for Joe outside the lunchroom.

Joe sauntered over to join them. He was acting like a cop in a TV show. He talked from the side of his mouth. "They inside yet?" he asked.

Frank nodded. "Yeah," he muttered. "Ready?"

Chet made a noise like a siren. The three friends stalked into the lunchroom. Zack and his group were at their usual table in the corner.

"Hey, look who's here," Zack said loudly. "It's the Boy De*fec*tives and their sidekick. I'll bet they're on a big case."

His friend Brett grinned. "Sure," he said.

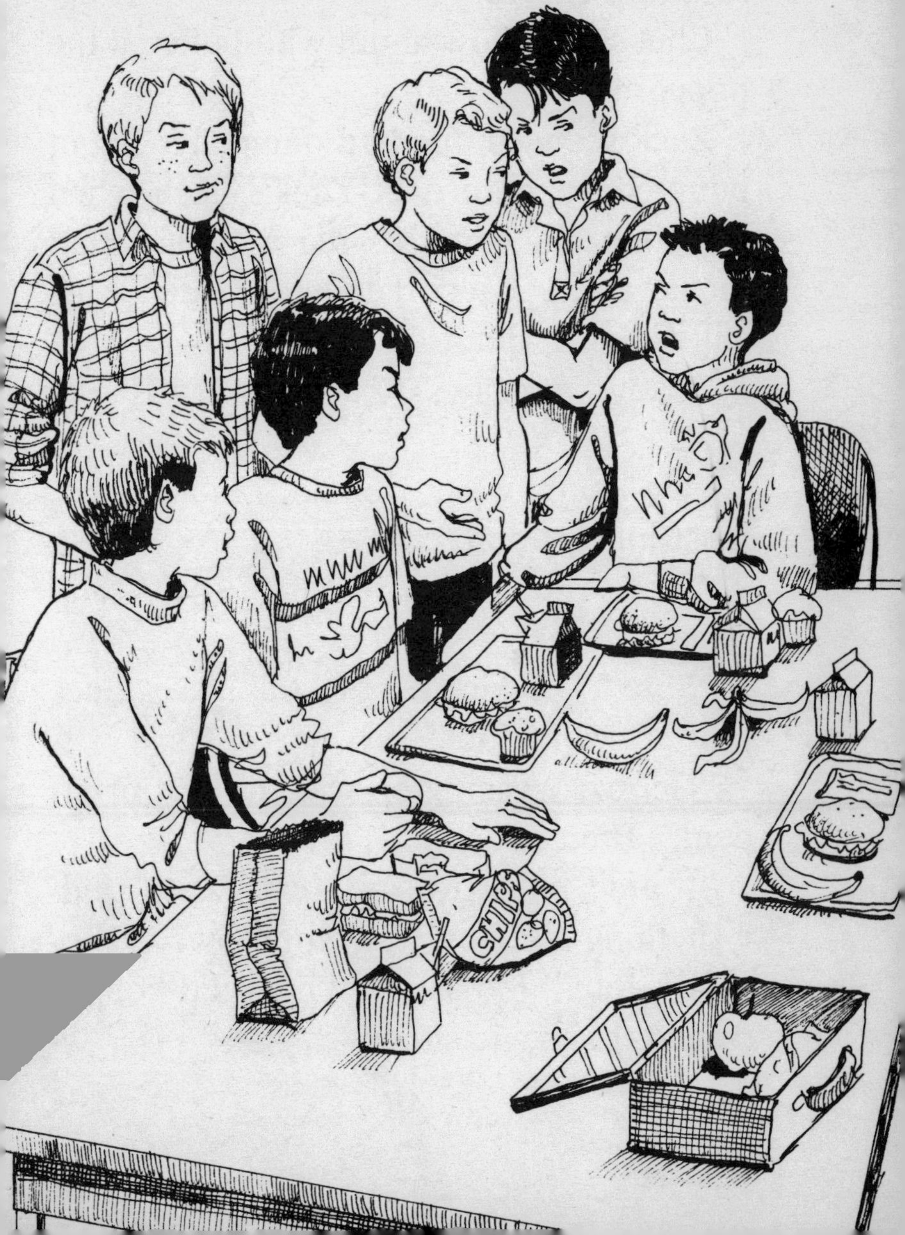
CHIPS

"Like who stole the cheese from the macaroni and cheese."

Chet said, "How about who buttered the popcorn?"

Zack scowled. Joe had dumped a bag of buttered popcorn over Zack's head when everyone had gone to see a Jimmy Han movie at the Bayport movie theater. Kids still laughed about that.

"Okay, wiseguy," Zack said. "You're next."

"We don't want trouble," Frank said. "Just information."

"We've got lots of that," Zack said. "Right, guys?"

"Sure," Dribbles Libretti said. "Six times four is twenty-four."

"George Washington was the first president," Brett added.

"It ain't polite to say *ain't*," Zack said. "Anything else you want to know?"

"Uh-huh," Joe said. "Where did you sit during the magic show?"

"You know where I was," Zack replied. "I was on the couch. You were on the floor in front of me."

"Was anybody next to you?" Frank asked.

"Sure. Biff was," Zack said. "You guys got a problem with that?"

"But I saw Biff standing at the back," Chet said.

Zack glared at him. "So what?" he said. "Biff got bored, like me. That magic show stunk. So he got up and walked around."

"But you were still sitting down?" Joe asked.

"Yup," Zack said. "What's it to you, anyway?"

"Somebody took Brian's videotape. Somebody hid it," Frank said. "That wasn't nice. It spoiled Brian's birthday party. Whoever it was shouldn't get away with it."

"Hey, guys," Zack said. "I learned a

magic trick at Brian's party. Want to see?"

"Sure," Chet said. "What is it?"

Zack stood up. He took his milk container from his tray.

"Abracadabra!" he said. Then he poured the milk into Chet's shirt pocket.

6

Advice from a Pro

Chet let out a yell. His shirt was soaked. He lunged forward and tried to tackle Zack. Zack backed away. He was laughing.

Chet followed. "You creep!" he shouted. "Look what you did!"

Frank jumped between the two. "That was really mean," he told Zack. Zack sneered at him.

Mr. Levy was lunchroom monitor on Mondays. He hurried over. "What's going on here?" he demanded.

"Zack poured milk on Chet," Joe said.

Zack spread his hands and shrugged. "I don't get it," he said in an innocent voice. "I saw a magician do that the other day. So I tried it. But it didn't work."

Mr. Levy looked at Chet's shirt. "It certainly didn't," he said. "Okay, Zack, off to Ms. Vaughn's office. You can explain to her."

"I didn't do—" Zack started to say.

"Move it!" Mr. Levy said.

Zack strutted off, smirking.

"Chet, do you have anything else to wear?" Mr. Levy asked.

"I have a T-shirt in my cubby," Chet said.

"Okay, go change." Mr. Levy turned to Frank and Joe. "What started this ruckus?"

"We just asked Zack some questions," Frank said.

"About something that happened Saturday," Joe added. "We thought he might know something about it."

"Detecting again?" Mr. Levy said. "Okay, but stay away from Zack and his friends. I don't want more trouble."

Tanya was sitting nearby. Joe and Frank went over. "Zack is such a bully," she said. "We should tell Sensei."

Sensei was the name karate students called their teacher.

"You're right. He'll know what to do," Frank said. "Listen, Tanya. Do you remember who was near you during the magic show?"

"Still on the case?" She wrinkled her forehead as she thought. "Well, Brian was sitting next to me."

"Which side?" Joe asked.

"The left," Tanya replied. "And Jennifer was on the other side."

Frank wrote down what she'd said.

"Your Jimmy Han collection is famous," Joe said. "Wouldn't you love to have that tape in it?"

Tanya frowned. "You suspect me? Here. Let me show you something."

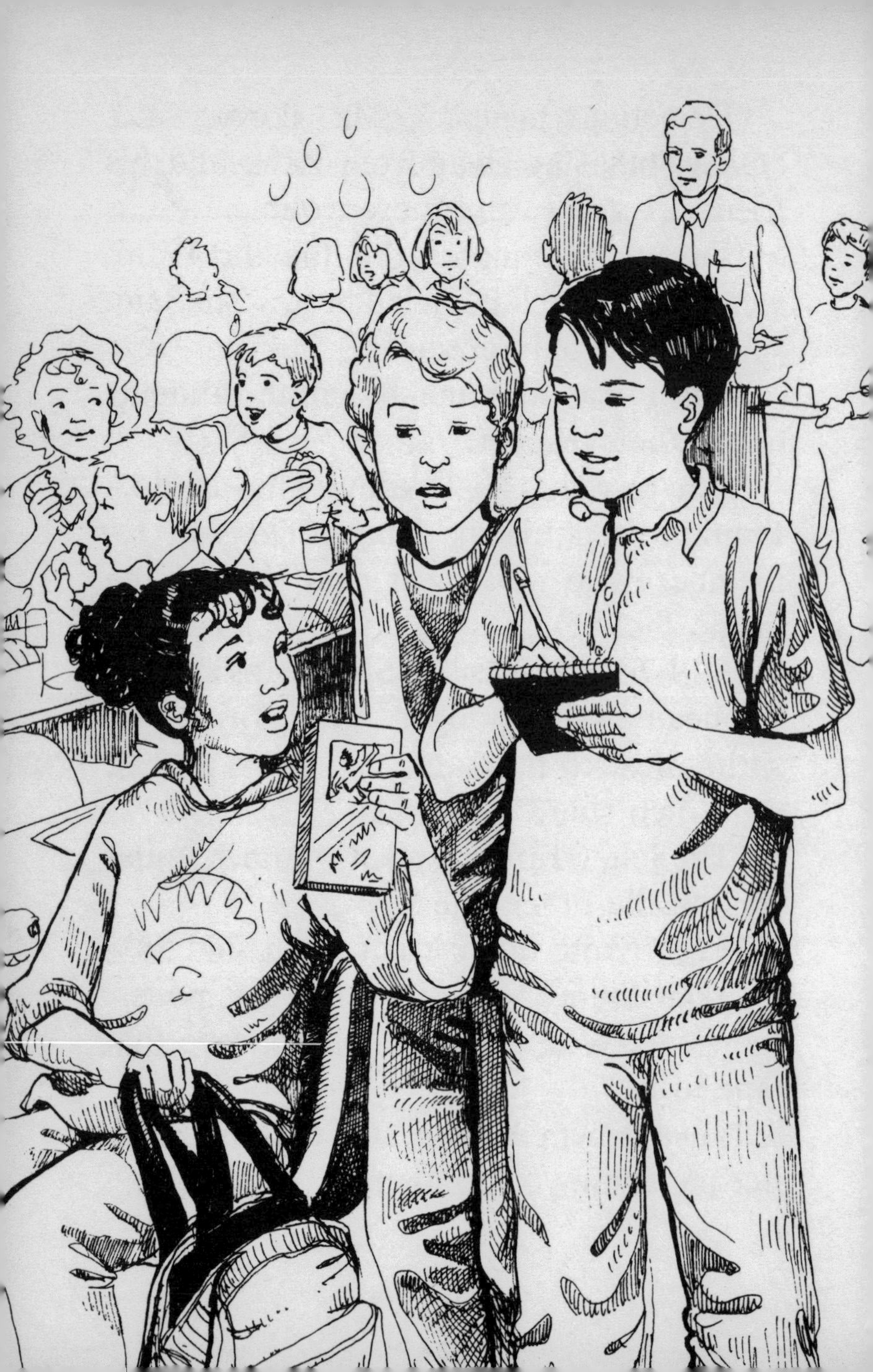

She opened her backpack. There was a videocassette inside. The label read, *The Dragon's Cave.* "My mom has a friend who works at the company that made the movie," Tanya said. "That's how I knew about the movie. I had already seen it. I couldn't tell anyone at the party. It would have spoiled Brian's present."

"So you had no reason to steal Brian's cassette," Joe said.

"No reason at all," Tanya said. "And stealing is against the code of the warrior. Ask Sensei. He'll tell you."

After school Frank and Chet met Joe out front. Iola came running up.

"What are we going to do now?" she asked.

"You could go play with your little friends," Chet suggested.

"It's more fun being a detective," Iola said.

"There's one suspect we haven't questioned," Frank said. "Jennifer."

"I know where she lives," Iola said. "It's near the park. We could walk there."

Jennifer lived in a brick house that overlooked the park. They rang the bell. A boy who Joe thought looked about twelve answered.

"Jennifer's not home yet," he said. "She and Brian get home from their school later than we do."

"We know her from karate class," Joe said.

"Come in." The boy held the door wider. "I'm Josh. I'll bet you're all Jimmy Han fans. Me, too. Isn't he awesome? Jennifer promised she'd get me his latest movie."

They followed Josh inside. Joe caught Frank's eye. Josh's statement was real evidence. How could Jennifer get *The Dragon's Cave* . . . unless she stole it?

A yellow school bus stopped outside. Jennifer hopped out and ran up the front walk. "Hi," she said when she walked inside. "What brings you guys here?"

"A few questions," Frank said. "About Brian's party—and the missing video." He pulled a notebook from his backpack and started to take notes.

"You think I tried to steal his video," Jennifer said. She laughed. "I thought about taking it. But it wouldn't have been right. Besides, I couldn't figure out how to do it.

"Anyway, look," she added. She reached into her backpack and pulled out a cassette. "Brian watched it last night. Then he decided to lend it to me. He gave it to me in school today. Here, Josh."

Joe and Frank exchanged another look. It seemed that Jennifer wasn't a suspect either. Who did that leave? Joe wondered.

"Who was sitting near you during the magic show?" Joe asked Jennifer.

"I was on the end," she replied. "Tanya was next to me. Oh, and Zack was standing in front of me for part of it. He kept blocking my view."

"Which part?" Frank asked. He was taking notes again.

"The second half," Jennifer said. "After the lights came back on."

"Did you leave your seat during the show?" Chet asked.

Jennifer shook her head. "Nope. Ask Tanya. She was there the whole time, too."

On the walk home, Iola said, "I just thought of something funny. When the show started, Biff was next to me on the couch. Rudy was on the floor in front. But at the end, Rudy was on the couch. And I don't remember them changing places."

"Where was Biff at the end?" Joe asked.

"I don't know," Iola said.

"Standing at the back," Chet said. "I saw him there."

"Why couldn't everyone stay in one place?" Joe said. "I'm getting confused."

"We'll straighten it out," Frank promised. "Maybe Dad can help."

At the Hardys' driveway, Chet and Iola said good-bye and continued walking to their home. Joe and Frank went inside. Fenton Hardy was in his study. They explained their problem.

Their father rubbed his chin as he listened. "A map of the room would help," he said. "And you need to make a timetable. You have to figure out where everyone was and when."

"How? We didn't look at our watches," Frank said.

Mr. Hardy smiled. "You don't have to be that exact," he said. "Choose the important moments. For each person, jot down where he or she was and how you know. Like this."

He showed them what he meant. He drew a picture of the den that they were standing in. He drew a small rectangle to show the desk. Then he drew a small circle to show the chair he was sitting in. On the chair, he put a large *X*, and wrote "Dad" next to it. Then he put two *X*'s next to the chair and wrote "Frank" and "Joe" beside them.

"Thanks, Dad," Frank said.

"We knew we could count on you," Joe added as they rushed upstairs to their bedrooms.

Drawing a map of Brian's movie room didn't take long. Figuring out where everybody had been at different times was a lot harder.

Finally the timetable was filled in. Frank and Joe studied it.

"Everyone sure kept moving around a lot," Joe said. "Like Biff. First he was on the couch, then at the back of the room, then by the door."

"Do you know what that means?" Frank said with excitement.

"I sure do," Joe said. "There's only one kid who could have turned out the lights—Biff Hooper!"

7

Face-off at the Dojo

We know Biff turned out the lights," Frank said. "But he couldn't have taken the cassette. You know what we need? To question everybody, all at once."

"How?" Joe asked. "Mr. Levy told us to keep away from Zack. And Brian and Jennifer don't even go to our school."

"They're all in karate class, though," Frank said. "Let's call. Maybe Sensei will let us have a meeting after class tomorrow."

Their instructor wasn't at the Bayport

Karate School that evening. Frank talked to Bobby Lee, the director. He explained what he and Joe wanted to do.

"Sensei has responsibility for the class," Bobby said. "But I'll tell him your request. I think he'll agree. Righting wrongs is an important goal of the martial arts."

Frank thanked him and hung up. Next, Joe called the Great Merlino. The magician listened to the plan. "I wouldn't miss it," he said. "It sounds as if the Clues Brothers are staging a magic show of their own!"

The students bowed to each other. Then they faced the front and bowed to Sensei. Karate class was over.

Usually the students got their things from the cubby room and went home. Not today. Everyone knew that something different was about to happen.

Sensei raised a hand. "Frank and Joe Hardy asked if they could talk with you," he said. "Joe? Frank?"

Frank and Joe walked to the front.

"We've been trying to find out what happened at Brian's party the other day," Frank began.

Zack interrupted. "We're all sick of Brian's party," he said. He started toward the door. "I'm leaving."

"Fine. Go," Joe said. "But you'll never know what people said about you."

Zack stopped. He glared at Joe and Frank. Then he came back to the group.

"You all remember what happened," Frank said. "During the magic show, somebody turned off the lights. While the lights were out, Merlino's magic bag vanished. Brian's videotape vanished, too."

"They were found, though," Tanya said.

Joe nodded. "Right. I found the bag under the sofa."

"And I found the video, inside the sofa," Iola said.

A movement at the back of the karate studio caught Frank's eye. Merlino had just come in. Brian's dad was with him.

"So, who turned out the lights?" Frank asked.

"Who knows?" Zack muttered. "Who cares?"

Frank ignored him. "We made a time-table," he said. "It tells where everybody was at different times. Joe?"

Joe held up the timetable. "Take when the lights went out," he said. "Most of us were sitting down, watching the show. One guy wasn't, though. He was at the back of the room, next to the light switches. Right, Biff?"

"You're full of hot air," Biff growled.

Joe grinned. "Maybe I am. But you were there, weren't you? And you switched off the lights."

Biff glanced around. He looked trapped. "What if I did?" he said. "It was just a joke. It doesn't mean I stole anything."

"No, it doesn't," Frank said. "But some-body took Merlino's bag. Somebody who *knew* the lights were about to go out. Who did you tell, Biff?"

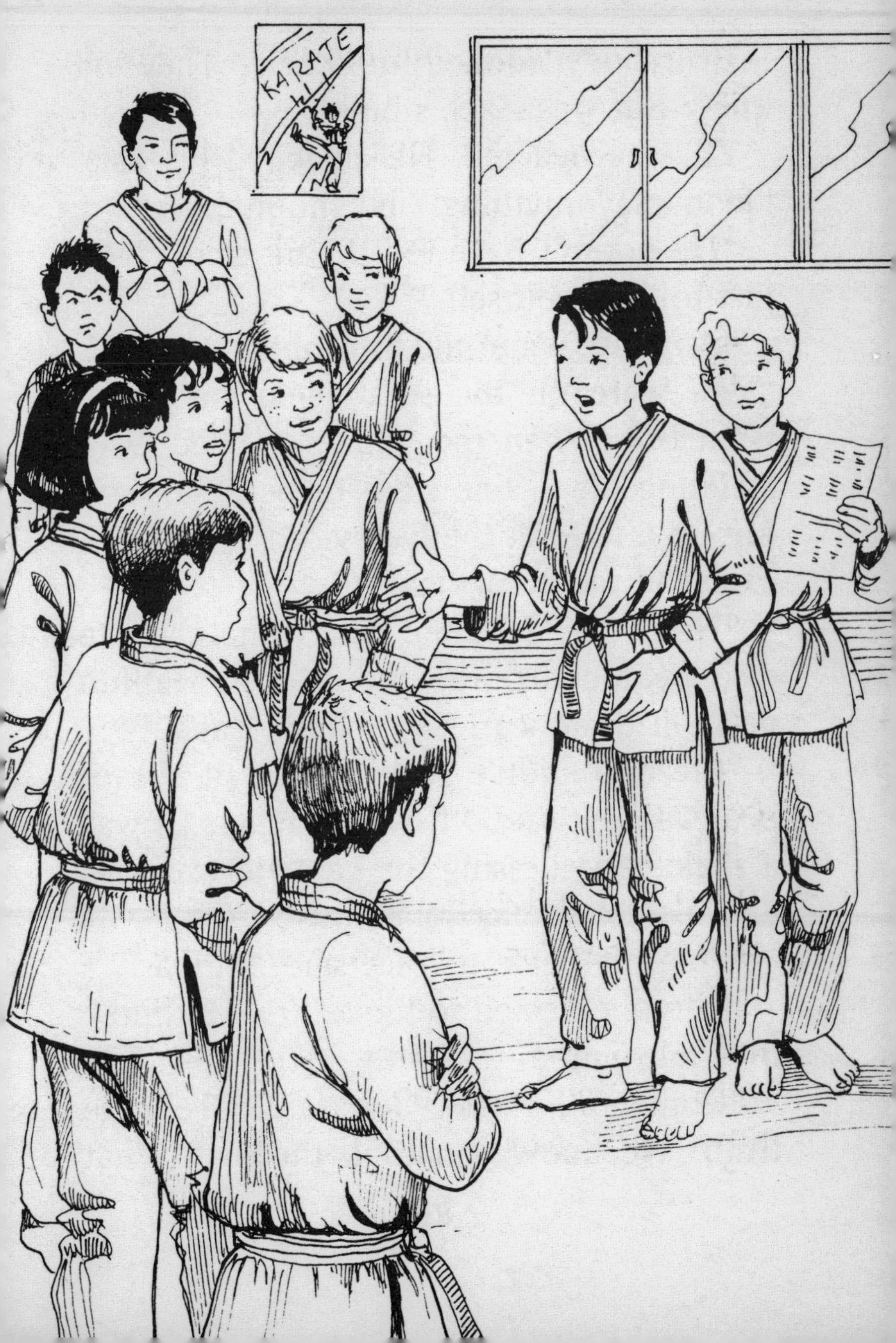
KARATE

Everybody looked at Zack. They all knew Biff was Zack's buddy.

Zack turned red. He clenched his fists. "Don't say anything!" he shouted.

"He doesn't have to," Frank said. "You just told us yourself."

"Anyway, it's in the timetable," Joe said. "You were on the sofa when the lights went out. When they came on, you were standing off to one side. In between, you ran up and took the bag with the cassette. You had plenty of time."

"Hold on," Jennifer said. "The cassette disappeared before, didn't it? Merlino *made* it disappear. Why blame Zack?"

"Merlino didn't really make it disappear," Frank said. "It wasn't magic. It was a trick. I'm guessing the cassette was hidden inside the bag somehow."

From the back, a voice said, "It was."

Everyone turned to look. "It's Merlino," they murmured.

"Come on, Zack," Joe said. "Tell the truth. We know you took the bag. What then? You didn't hide the cassette. You couldn't. Somebody tucked it into the sofa. But you didn't go back there."

Zack scowled. He ran his fingers through his spiky hair. "Okay, look," he said. "I was sore at Merlino. He made me look like an idiot."

"That's not hard," somebody whispered loudly.

Zack turned and glared. Then he said, "Besides, I thought it'd be funny. The vanishing bag vanishes. Get it? I was going to say a magic word and make it reappear. I didn't even think about Brian's videotape. I wanted to watch it, same as everybody else."

"What happened?" Frank asked.

"I was all ready when the lights went out," Zack said. "I ran to the front and grabbed the bag. Then I ran back. But in the dark I tripped over somebody sitting on the floor. I dropped the bag. I wanted to hunt for it. But I was scared the lights would go back on. So I left it there."

"In the middle of the floor?" Chet said. "I doubt it. How did it get to the sofa?"

"I don't know, wimp," Zack said. "And I don't care. You've heard all I've got to say."

"Then who hid the cassette?" Tanya asked. "It didn't jump into the sofa by itself. Even a Jimmy Han movie isn't that active!"

Frank laughed along with the others. Then he said, "Let's look at our timetable. Who did Zack trip over? Who was sitting on the floor?"

Joe studied the timetable. "There was Frank and me. Amanda. Rudy. And Michael. That's before the lights went out. And when the lights came on, all of us were *still* there. All except—"

"Rudy!" Iola shouted. "Remember? I told you. Rudy came over to the sofa!"

8

The Secret Revealed

Rudy was standing near the back of the karate studio. Everyone turned to stare at him. Joe thought he looked ready to run out the door.

Sensei said, "Rudy, the truth is very important."

"I—I," Rudy stammered. "I didn't mean to. Not really. It just . . ."

"What happened, Rudy?" Joe asked. He tried to sound friendly, so that Rudy wouldn't feel bad.

"I didn't like being in the dark," Rudy

began. "Then somebody bumped into me hard. He hurt my leg. The bag landed in my lap, and the cassette fell out."

"How did you know what it was?" Frank asked.

"I know what a cassette feels like," Rudy told him. "Besides, I felt bad because Merlino never called on me. I'd thought of taking the cassette myself. But I wouldn't have done it, honest."

"Then why did you hide it in the sofa?" Iola asked.

"I was scared people would say I took it. So I jumped up and stuck it under the cushions. Then I sat down to hide it. I guess I kicked the bag under the couch at the same time. And once everybody started looking, I was too scared to say anything."

"Rudy, it was wrong to hide the cassette," Sensei said. "But it was brave of you to tell us about it." He bowed to Rudy. Rudy gulped and bowed back.

Brian's father came forward with Merlino. "I'm glad to know what happened," he said. "And especially glad to know that Merlino was in no way at fault. He's a fine young man and an exciting performer."

"I might know a few tricks," Merlino said. "The real magicians here are Bayport's favorite detectives. Let's have a big hand for Joe and Frank Hardy—the Clues Brothers!"

It was Wednesday afternoon. Frank and Joe had rushed home from school.

"Do you think he'll come?" Joe asked.

"Of course he will," Frank said. "He said he would."

Just then the doorbell rang. They dashed to the door and pulled it open.

"Hi, guys," Merlino said. "All ready for your first lesson?"

"You bet," they shouted. They led Merlino into the living room.

Merlino unzipped his backpack. "Here's the first thing a student of magic has to learn. Never ever tell the audience how you did a trick. They'll beg you to, but don't do it. If you do, you'll just spoil their fun. You'll also ruin that trick for other magicians. Okay?"

Frank and Joe nodded.

"Good," Merlino said. "Today we're going to work on a trick you already know." He grinned. From his backpack he pulled out a black velvet bag—*the* black velvet bag.

"Oh, no," Joe groaned. "That again!"

Merlino reached inside and turned the bag inside out. "As you see, it's empty," he said. "Or is it?"

He pushed it right side out. When he took his hand out, he was holding a bunch of flowers.

"Wow!" Joe said. "Did you have that up your sleeve?"

Merlino smiled. "Sometimes I keep things up my sleeve," he said. "But not this time. Hand me that rabbit."

He was pointing to a little china bunny on the lamp table. Frank gave it to him. Merlino dropped it into the bag. Then he

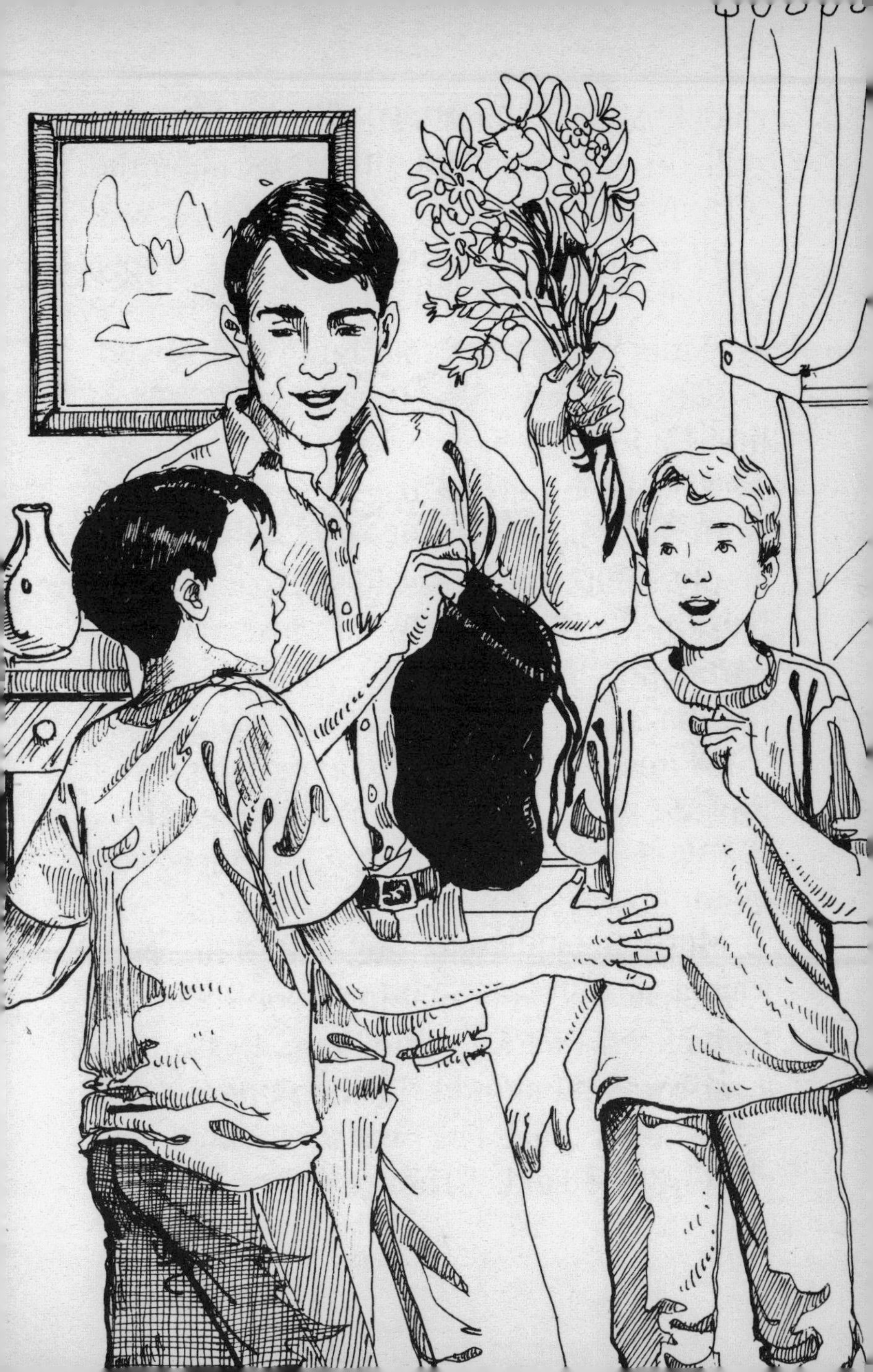

said, "Abracadabra." He reached in and pulled the bag inside out. It was empty.

"What about your hand?" Frank asked.

Merlino opened his hand. It was empty, too.

"Mom really likes that bunny," Joe said.

"Don't worry. She'll get it back," Merlino told him.

"Can I look at the bag?" Frank asked.

Merlino handed it to him. It was still empty. But Frank could feel something hard in the bottom. "There's a secret compartment," he said. "It's as if there are *two* bags."

Joe reached into the compartment and pulled out the bunny. "Ta-daa!" he said.

"It's simple," Frank said, "once you know how it's done."

"Most magic tricks are," Merlino said. "The real skill is in making it look natural. I practiced this trick for hours in front of a mirror. You should do the same."

He took the bag back. "Watch me closely," he said. "Then each of you try.

I'll give you some hints. By our next lesson, you should be pretty good at it."

"You mean we can borrow the bag?" Joe exclaimed. "Yippee!"

"That's great," Frank said. "But what if Chet sees us with it? What if he asks how it works?"

"Easy," Joe said. He grinned. "We just tell him, 'I don't have a clue!'"

Do your younger brothers and sisters want to read books like yours?

Let them know there are books just for them!

THE NANCY DREW NOTEBOOKS®

#1 The Slumber Party Secret
#2 The Lost Locket
#3 The Secret Santa
#4 Bad Day for Ballet
#5 The Soccer Shoe Clue
#6 The Ice Cream Scoop
#7 Trouble at Camp Treehouse
#8 The Best Detective
#9 The Thanksgiving Surprise
#10 Not Nice on Ice
#11 The Pen Pal Puzzle
#12 The Puppy Problem
#13 The Wedding Gift Goof
#14 The Funny Face Fight
#15 The Crazy Key Clue
#16 The Ski Slope Mystery
#17 Whose Pet Is Best?
#18 The Stolen Unicorn
#19 The Lemonade Raid
#20 Hannah's Secret
#21 Princess on Parade
#22 The Clue in the Glue
#23 Alien in the Classroom
#24 The Hidden Treasures
#25 Dare at the Fair

Look for a brand-new story every other month

Available from Minstrel® Books
Published by Pocket Books   1356-01